WHAT TO SAY TO CLARA

What To Say To CLARA

Barney Saltzberg

Atheneum New York 1984

For Barbara Bottner
A special thanks to Gary Bardovi

Library of Congress Cataloging in Publication Data

Saltzberg, Barney.
What to say to Clara.

SUMMARY: Eric thinks the new girl at school is the
most wonderful person he's ever seen, but every time
he gets near her, he doesn't know what to say.
[1. Firendship—Fiction.   2. Schools—Fiction]
I. Title.
PZ7.S1552Wh   1984   [E]   83-15567

Text and pictures copyright © 1984 by Barney Saltzberg
All rights reserved
Published simultaneously in Canada by
McClelland & Stewart, Ltd.
Type set by Linotype Composition, New York City
Printed and bound by
the Worzalla Publishing Company, Stevens Point, Wisconsin
Typography by Mary Ahern
First Edition

Today in school, Mr. Tweeds introduced a new girl to our class.
Her name is Clara.

Everybody whooped and hollered...
except for me.

Mr. Tweeds gave Clara the one and only empty seat in the room.

Right next to me.

My stomach did a handstand.

I wanted to say something, but what?

Then I had to spell refrigerator, but couldn't.

I was busy thinking about what to say to Clara.

At lunch, Trudy and Alice and Peter
talked with Clara.
I wished I could think
of something to say.

I wondered if she liked to dance.

Or if she liked space movies.

On my way home from school, I thought if I brought
her a present I wouldn't have to say anything.
So I got her some chocolate-covered raisins.
But by the time I was home there were only three left.

Later that night I got an idea of what to say to Clara.

I practiced with Cromwell.

He didn't go for it.

The next day I knew I had to say something to Clara.

But I always picked the wrong time to try.

That afternoon my mother got a letter in the mail
and I had another idea.

I waited until after dinner.
I put on my favorite pair of cactus pajamas
and sat down to write Clara a letter.
I got as far as, "Dear Clara."
After that, everything I wrote sounded funny.

The idea wasn't working.

So I gave up and went
to bed.
And began to dream.

When I woke up
I felt better.

I knew what
to say to Clara.

I practiced all the way to school.

Just to make sure it sounded right.

When I saw Clara, she was talking to Jody Lake.
I thought I better wait until Clara was by herself
before I said anything.

I hoped she didn't see me go by.

My knees felt weak when I saw
Clara by herself. I stopped her
anyway.

Date Due

Code 4386-04, CLS-4, Broadman Supplies, Nashville, Tenn.,
Printed in U.S.A.